Copyright © 1995, 2004 and 2005
by John D. Caporale, Ph.D..          28136-CAPO
Library of Congress Number:          2005904050
ISBN:          Softcover          1-4134-9493-5

This is a work of fiction. Names, characters, places and incidents either are the product of the author's imagination or are used fictitiously, and any resemblance to any actual persons, living or dead, events, or locales is entirely coincidental.

This book was printed in the United States of America.

To order additional copies of this book, contact:
Xlibris Corporation
1-888-795-4274
www.Xlibris.com
Orders@Xlibris.com

# THEY CALL ME CHICKEN

## A Story of Courage

by John D. Caporale, Ph.D.

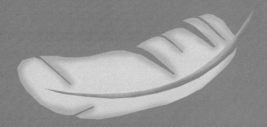

Illustrated by Wendy Hannibal Summers

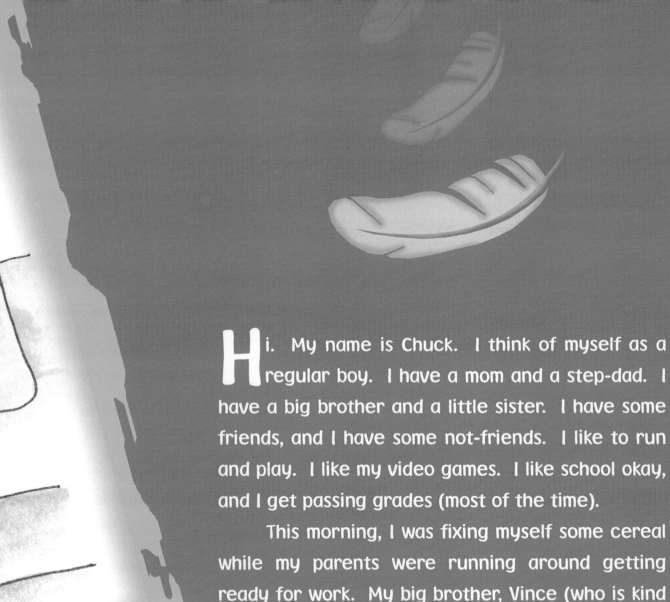

Hi. My name is Chuck. I think of myself as a regular boy. I have a mom and a step-dad. I have a big brother and a little sister. I have some friends, and I have some not-friends. I like to run and play. I like my video games. I like school okay, and I get passing grades (most of the time).

This morning, I was fixing myself some cereal while my parents were running around getting ready for work. My big brother, Vince (who is kind of mean), came into the kitchen.

"Hey, Shorty!" he snapped. "I need some money!"

"So?" I said, pouring my milk.

"So go ahead and grab me some money from Mom's purse," he whispered, an ugly, menacing sneer on his ugly, menacing face. He pointed to her purse that lay open on the counter. Mom always had a few dollar bills stuffed in her purse. "She'll never know," he rasped when I didn't move.

"No way!" I told him.

"Just do it," Vince said. "Are you chicken?"

"No," I explained. "I don't steal. If you want to do something wrong, do it yourself!" Heck, I said to myself, I'd rather be a chicken than a thief any day. Vince scowled and shot me a withering glare. He stepped over to Mom's purse and looked in, without touching it. Then he looked side to side, checking for Mom or Dad. No sign of them. I heard him mumble something about me being a chicken then he skulked away without taking anything.

Hmm, let's see?  I stood up to him. Then he wouldn't do what he called me a chicken for refusing to do.  I obviously had more courage than him.

I finished getting ready for school. My mom called me when my friends came to the door. I always walk to school with Ralph, Danny and Steve. I was going to tell them about Vince, but then I decided it wasn't that important. So I shrugged it off and rushed through the door, ready to face the day's challenges.

"Bye, Mom!" I yelled, the door slamming shut behind me. I greeted my friends and off we went to school.

We started talking about what we saw on TV last night and about what Miss Carter was going to have us do in class. About half way there, Ralph suddenly stopped.

"Hey, guys," he said. "Why should we go to school? Let's skip school and go fishing."

We just stood there. Nobody said anything.

"I don't think that's a good idea," I finally said. Danny and Steve still didn't say anything. I bet they didn't want to get in trouble any more than I did.

Ralph looked at me. "Why not? Are you a chicken?"

"No," I replied, calmly. "You know we would be caught, and I don't want to get in trouble. Besides, if I miss class, I'll fall behind and have a bunch of work to catch up."

"Chuck the Chicken!" howled Ralph.

I was thinking *How does standing up to you make me a chicken?* when Steve spoke up. "Chuck's right, Ralph. I don't want to get in trouble either."

"Yeah," added Danny. "Let's just go to school."

I knew Steve and Danny didn't want to play hooky, but they're sometimes too scared to speak up, at least until somebody else says something first. A lot of people are like that.

Ralph thought about it a second and then sighed. "Oh, all right. I'm sorry I called you a chicken, Chuck."

Then we headed for school.

I didn't always have the courage to stand up for myself. I remember one time when I ran into a bunch of guys I knew who were smoking cigarettes. They offered me one and when I said no thanks, they started calling me a chicken. I didn't know what I know now so I got embarrassed and mad, and I smoked a cigarette. It was horrible, exactly like eating smoke, and it scorched my throat. I didn't want to be called a chicken so I forced myself to smoke the whole thing. Then I threw up in front of everybody. They laughed so hard I wanted to punch them, but I couldn't even stand up.

I realized then that there was no courage in smoking that cigarette, only stupidity. Courage would have come from sticking to my "No, thanks." But to top it all off, my parents somehow found out about it and flipped out! I got yelled at for an hour and grounded for a month! I was the only one at school to miss the big skating party. Man, I was mad!

Every once in a while I still get suckered by someone, but the more I practice my courage, the more I have.

Class was okay. Then came lunch, then recess. Steve and I were over by some trees, tossing the football back and forth. An older boy I'd never seen before suddenly appeared out of the trees by me. He blocked the way so Steve couldn't throw me the ball.

"Hey, man," he said, all friendly-like. "You look like a cool kid. I got something cool for you."

"What?" I asked.

"Something that will make you feel *great*! And it ain't no cereal." He held out his hand, and I saw different colored pills laying in his palm. He was trying to make me take drugs.

"No, thanks," I told him.

"You're nothin' but a chicken!" he exclaimed. "You must be a chicken."

"If you mean by 'chicken' that I'm scared, then you're right!" I said. "Of course I'm scared to take drugs and turn my brain to fried eggs! I'm scared to jump out of an airplane without a parachute, too!" He had my dander up. "I'm smart enough to be scared of something any intelligent person would be scared of."

Then I ran like the wind. Steve, having heard the whole thing, blew by me.

We were both smart enough to know when we *should* be scared of something!

The bell finally rang and school was out. It was only Steve and me walking home together. As soon as we stepped out of sight of the school, I heard a voice behind me shout my name. We stopped. I turned.

"Is that who I think it is?" Steve mumbled to me under his breath.

"It is," I said, dismally.

It was Greg, our friendly neighborhood class bully. He was big, he was ugly, and he was mean. He had his little ugly, mean crony with him.

"Are you ready to get your face pounded?" Greg snarled, making him look even uglier, kind of like a bulldog with its face turned inside out.

"Let's go," I said quietly to Steve.

We turned our backs to Greg, which is a dangerous thing to do (not to mention courageous), but it had to be done. I still felt a little scared. My heart was pounding pretty hard. We started walking, acting as casually as possible. The best thing to do with a bully (if possible) is ignore him. You see, bullies really love to hear themselves talk. They think it makes them tough. If you ignore them, they get to talk more (which they love, by the way) but then they shut up because they realize nobody's listening.

"Chuck, you're a chicken!" yelled Greg, standing where he was. "Come on and fight me, you big chicken!" Then he started with the chicken noises. "Bawk! Bawk! Chuck is a chicken! Bawk! Bawk!" Flapping his arms like a chicken, he sure looked like a goofball. I tried not to laugh.

"Doesn't that make you mad?" asked Steve.

"Sure it does," I agreed. "But fighting him isn't going to stop it. Fact is, I would probably just get hurt, and I'm choosing not to get hurt just because some moron I don't even care about calls me a chicken. He'll stop if I ignore him." Greg calling me a chicken sure doesn't make me one, especially when I have to be brave to walk away from him.

And sure enough. By the time I was done talking, Greg had shut up. In fact, he was no where in sight. He probably ran off to bully someone who would play his game.

We stopped at the little convenience store that a lot of the kids from school hang out at. I bought us each a candy bar. We stood around the store eating and talking to some other friends who were there. The store manager didn't like us just standing around inside, but we always did it anyway.

Steve suddenly pointed towards the door. I looked over and saw Penny and her friends Holly and Karen come through the door. Penny was the prettiest girl in school and, yes, like all the other boys, I had a crush on her. I counted myself lucky if she ever even talked to me.

"Hi, Chuck," she said, sweetly, batting her eyelashes.

I couldn't believe she was talking to me! I couldn't figure out why. Maybe she liked me! I'd have done anything for her to be my girlfriend. "Hi," I replied, still staring and in shock.

Penny said, "I'll walk home with you." All right! I thought. Then she finished, "If you get me some candy."

All right! Oh, no! Aargh!!! I couldn't believe it. I had no money! I'd just spent the little I had! "I'd love to," I said, but then confessed, "but I don't have any money." Disappointment wrung my heart.

"So? Just grab a chocolate bar and stick it in your pocket when no one's looking. I'll meet you outside and you can walk me home." She must have noticed my hesitance as she added, "I hope you're not chicken." She flashed a beautiful smile.

I thought about it. I honestly thought about it. I could probably get away with it and then Penny would like me. I did not want her to think I was a chicken. Then she'd never go out with me!

Then it struck me like a rock. She was calling me a chicken - like so many other kids do - just to get me to do what she wanted me to do. She didn't like me; she just liked chocolate and saw me as stupid enough to fall for her trick.

"Sorry," I said, shaking my head, making sure I sounded sad enough, "but you're not worth committing a crime for."

She glared at me and pronounced: "Chicken!" Then she stuck her nose up in the air and pranced off.

I watched as she tried the same thing on some other sap who would probably fall for it. I suddenly realized she was not nearly as pretty as I had thought.

"That was dumb," said Mark, one of the guys I was standing with. "You should have done it."

I sighed. Then I explained to the guys how I wasn't going to be tricked into doing something wrong; how I would rather be an honest "chicken" who does the right thing than a "brave" thief, even a brave thief with a pretty girlfriend.

Mark just gave me this look, but I could see the gears turning in his head, then the light bulb went on. "Geez," said Mark. "I guess you're right. You actually did the braver thing!" I noticed several of the guys were nodding their heads.

Well, what do you know? Most the of guys did understand that it took every ounce of courage I had to tell Penny no and that stealing for her would have been the chicken thing to do.

Mark had dropped the subject and we talked about whatever for a few minutes. Then Steve and I took off.

I arrived home to an empty house, which was probably just as well.  I grabbed a snack, left a note for my mom, and headed out again to meet Ralph, Danny and some of the guys.

We liked to hang out down by the river.  Sometimes we would play "King of the Mountain" on the hill.  I was king a lot. There is also a bridge where a train would cross the river.

The train came by frequently when we played there.  We always stopped to watch it pass, listening as the train made the bridge creak and quiver.

Suddenly, somebody dared Ralph to walk across the bridge, on the tracks.  Now Ralph is not one to turn down a dare, which is why they'd dared him to do it.  The people who dare someone to do something obviously know it is too dangerous, or too stupid, to do themselves.

Ralph scampered up the hill and stepped onto the tracks.  He looked a little nervous to me.  He started walking, slowly and carefully, stepping from tie to tie.

Finally, he reached the other side.  Then he turned and slowly came back this way.  He made it!  With a big smile, he bounced off the tracks.  He pointed to the boy who had dared him and said, "Now I dare you to do it!"

This other boy, Lou, suddenly paled, a look of terror striking his face, but just for an instant. He laughed and exclaimed, "I dare Chuck to do it! Let's get *him* to walk the bridge."

His dare was punctuated by several "yeah's" from other boys. I couldn't help but notice how Lou skillfully avoided having to do it by dumping the dare on me. But I wasn't about to do it. That train could come by anytime now. Fear is what tells smart people not to do something stupid.

"Forget it," I said. "You know how fast trains come up on that bridge."

"You're chicken!" Lou yelled. A couple of other boys echoed: "Chicken!" I wondered if Lou knew he was too scared to do it also.

"Forget it," I said again. "I'm not doing it."

Lou and a couple of others started in with strutting around like chickens, flapping their arms and making clucking noises.

I wished I had a video camera on me. I just stood there, waiting for them to finish because I knew they would. I felt a little sad, but I knew I could handle it.

A loud whistle abruptly pierced the air, and the train came speeding around the curve. A deadly serious silence descended upon us all as we froze, watching the train hit the bridge.

Then the rattle of the train rolling over the trestle shocked us into a flurry of motion, everyone doing something different, shrugging, walking away, staring off, anything not to think about it. We all knew that if I had taken the dare, I would have been smack dab in the middle of the bridge when the train came. Maybe lightning would have been fast enough to get off the bridge in time but not a human being.

I would have been crushed by the train or drowned in the river.

The train disappeared into the distance. Not another word of the dare or of being chicken was spoken. Lou appeared shaken. Soon we were all playing King of the Mountain.

I got home on time. "Hi, Mom. Hi, Angela," I said to my mom and my sister. Mom was getting dinner ready, and Angela was helping.

"Hi," they said at the same time. Mom asked me to help my little sister set the table so I did.

Soon Mom called out that dinner was ready, and Vince and our step-dad immediately appeared. Dinner was usual. We talked about school and what else we did today. I watched what I said because I didn't want to worry Mom, and I especially didn't want my step-dad criticizing me. Mom and Dad talked about grown-up stuff that didn't much interest me. My step-dad kept glaring at me in an odd way.

It gave me butterflies in my stomach because I know how he is.

We finished eating. I helped clean up. I did my homework, got ready for bed, and then went to watch TV until bedtime.

Bedtime came. I said goodnight to my mom, got my goodnight kiss on the cheek, and headed for my room.

"Chuck!" my step-dad yelled from his bedroom as I tried unsuccessfully to slip by unnoticed. "Come in here!" He sounded mad. But then when didn't he sound mad?

I stepped cautiously into his bedroom, feeling my stomach tighten with dread. I kept my head down and my mouth closed. Maybe I felt a little scared, but being smart isn't being chicken. And the smart thing with my step-dad was to keep your mouth shut and don't make eye contact. Kind of like dealing with a wild animal. And when I survived it, I felt good about being able to deal with it.

Gritting his teeth, he rasped, "Chuck, I understand you ran away from a fight after school."

35

"Sort of," I answered hesitantly.

"You did, Chuck. I can't believe a son of mine would do that even if you aren't my real son." He spoke in an angry tone of voice, but not yelling because he didn't want my mom to hear him talk to me like this. He continued, "You are a pathetic chicken, Chuck. I'm embarrassed to be your step-father."

I sighed heavily, my eyes looking at his feet. I felt like saying something, but I knew it wasn't any use. There are some people you just can't argue with because there is just no point. My step-dad just doesn't get it, and he never will. Fighting is wrong. And calling somebody names for choosing not to fight is wrong, too. It is especially bad when it's a parent who is supposed to be mature enough to know better. I sort of feel angry at my step-dad, but I feel more sorry for him that he is so immature and doesn't even know it. Still, it does hurt my feelings a little bit, even though I know I am right.

"Can I go to bed now?" I asked softly.

"Go to bed, Chicken!" he ordered.

I stepped into the hallway and paused to gather my thoughts. Then I grinned to myself, knowing that once again I had the courage and strength to do the right thing and feel good about it.

I lay in my bed, waiting to fall asleep and thinking. People can call me a chicken if they must. It doesn't really matter because I try to do what is right, and I know I am a good person. I don't like being called a chicken, but my real friends respect my choices. If someone thinks I'm a chicken, it does not make me one. They will never know the courage it takes to do the right thing. Sure, I'm scared sometimes. Everyone is, only some people are too scared to admit it. Having that courage makes me feel great because I know I have the courage to accomplish anything!

The end.

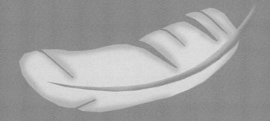